Text copyright © 2002 by Kate Banks
Pictures copyright © 2002 by Georg Hallensleben
All rights reserved
Distributed in Canada by Douglas & McIntyre Ltd.
Color separations by Hong Kong Scanner Arts
Printed and bound in the United States by Berryville Graphics
Designed by Nancy Goldenberg
First edition, 2002

Library of Congress Cataloging-in-Publication Data
Banks, Kate, 1960–
    Close your eyes / Kate Banks ; pictures by Georg Hallensleben.
      p.   cm.
    Summary: A mother tiger entices her child to sleep by telling of all that can be seen
with one's eyes closed.
    ISBN 0-374-31382-2
    [1. Tigers—Fiction.   2. Mother and child—Fiction.   3. Dreams—Fiction.   4. Sleep—
Fiction.]   I. Hallensleben, Georg, ill.   II. Title.

PZ7.B22594 Cl 2002
[E]—dc21

                                              99-46430

# Close Your Eyes

KATE BANKS   pictures by GEORG HALLENSLEBEN

Frances Foster Books • Farrar, Straus and Giroux • New York

The little tiger lay on his back in the tall grass.

The little tiger rolled onto his belly and listened
to the leaves quiver overhead.

"If I close my eyes, I can't see the tree," he said.

"But you can," said his mother. "You can see many
trees, where you can play hide-and-seek until
the night finds you and brings you home."

"Close your eyes, little tiger," said his mother, "and go to sleep."

But the little tiger didn't want to sleep.

"If I close my eyes," he said, "I can't see the sky."

"Yes, you can," said his mother, gently nudging him.
"You can even float among the clouds, and when night comes,
the moon will hold you in its lap."

"But I can't see the bird with the blue feathers,"
said the little tiger.

"If you close your eyes, you can see all kinds of birds
   with different feathers," said his mother.
"Maybe you can even fly."

The little tiger stretched his paws.

"But what if I fall?" he asked.

"I will be there to catch you," said his mother.

"And what if I get lost?" said the little tiger.
"Then I will find you," said his mother. "So close your eyes."

The little tiger closed his eyes. "It's dark," he said.
"Dark like your stripes," said his mother.

"I'm scared," said the little tiger.

"Don't be scared," said his mother.

"Dark is just the other side of light. It's what comes before dreams."

"Can I dream of the big mountains
where the rain lives?" asked the little tiger.

"Yes," said his mother. "And maybe you can dream of the desert, where there is no rain . . .

. . . or the ocean, which is as big as the blue sky."

. . . or the ocean, which is as big as the blue sky."

"Yes," said his mother. "And maybe you can dream
of the desert, where there is no rain . . .

"And when I open my eyes will the dreams be gone?"
asked the little tiger.

"Yes," said his mother, nestling up close to him.
"But I will be here. So close your eyes, little tiger."